ROBBIE'S BIG ADVENTURES

THE BEST SATURDAY EVER!

written by **GARY COOK**

illustrated by **ADAM SWARD**

MINNEAPOLIS, MINNESOTA

Published by Scarletta Kids, an imprint of Scarletta

Library of Congress Cataloging-in-Publication Data

Cook, Gary, 1959-
 The best Saturday ever! / by Gary Cook ; illustrated by Adam Sward. -- First edition.
     pages cm -- (Robbie's big adventures)
 Summary: On a rainy Saturday when the power goes off, Robbie manages to have fun using only his imagination.
 ISBN 978-1-938063-25-1 (hardcover : alk. paper) -- ISBN 978-1-938063-24-4 (nook kids book) -- ISBN 978-1-938063-23-7 (electronic)
 [1. Stories in rhyme. 2. Imagination--Fiction. 3. Play--Fiction.] I. Sward, Adam, illustrator. II. Title.
 PZ8.3.C7679Be 2013
 [E]--dc23
                                        2013008891

Book design by Mighty Media Inc., Minneapolis, MN

Printed and Manufactured in the United States
North Mankato, MN
Distributed by Publishers Group West

First edition

10 9 8 7 6 5 4 3 2 1

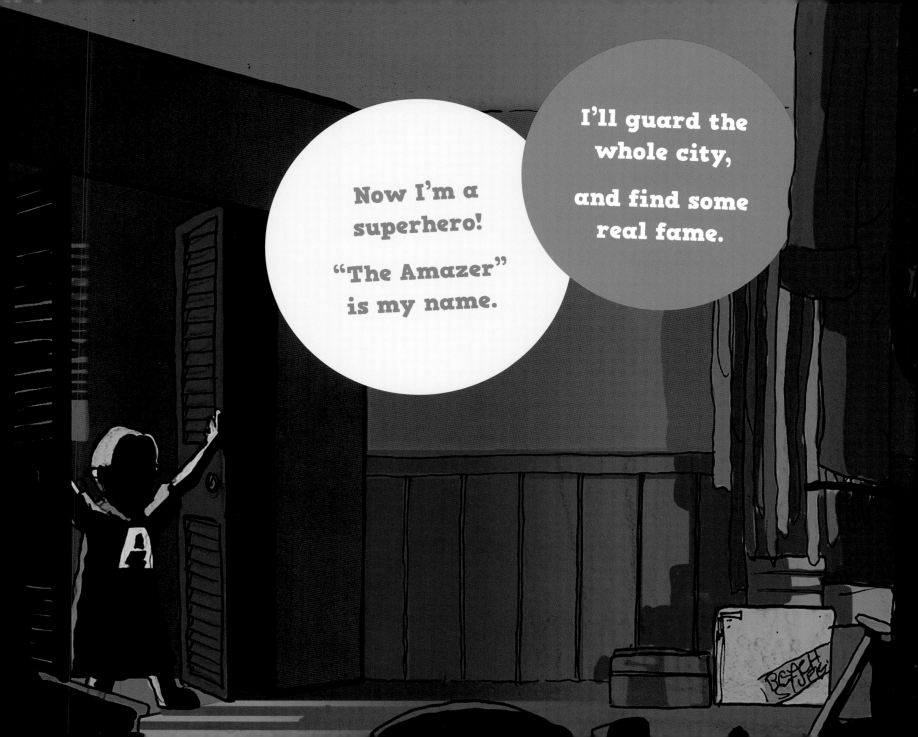

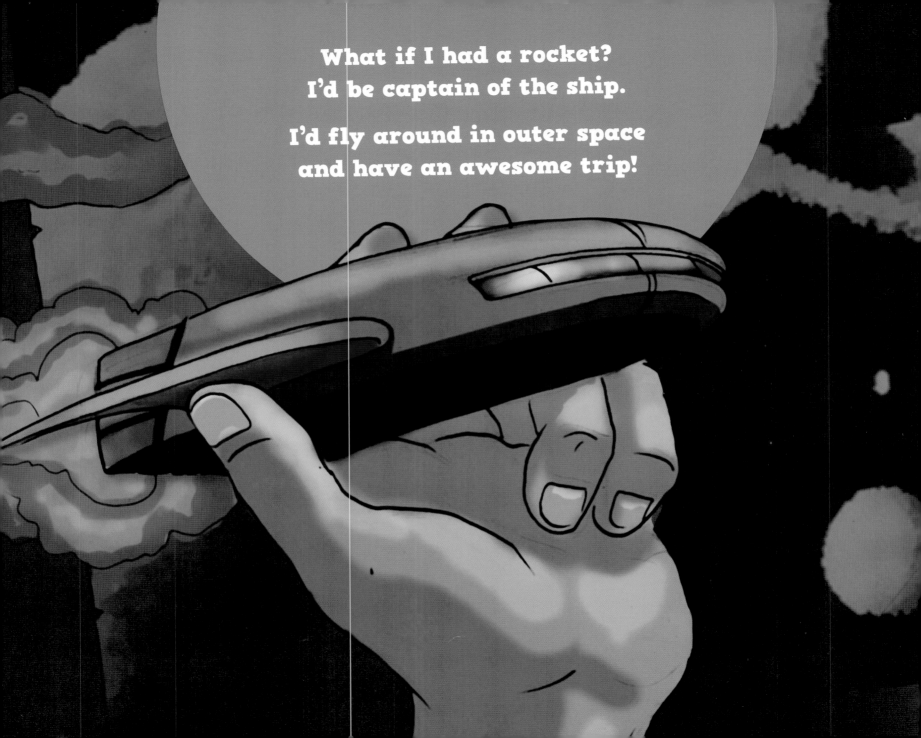

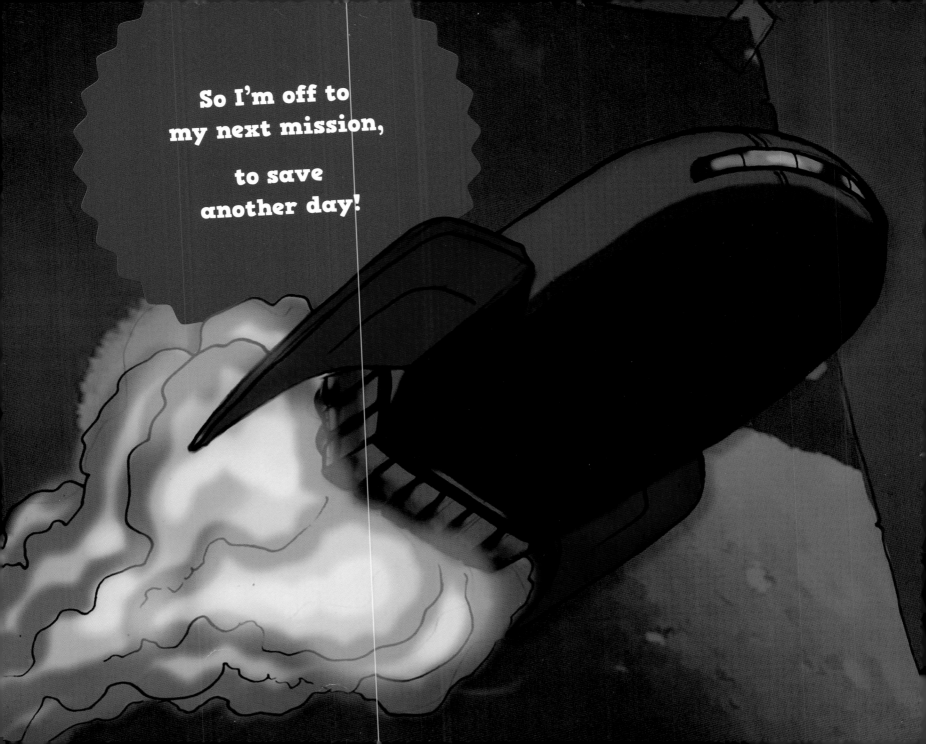

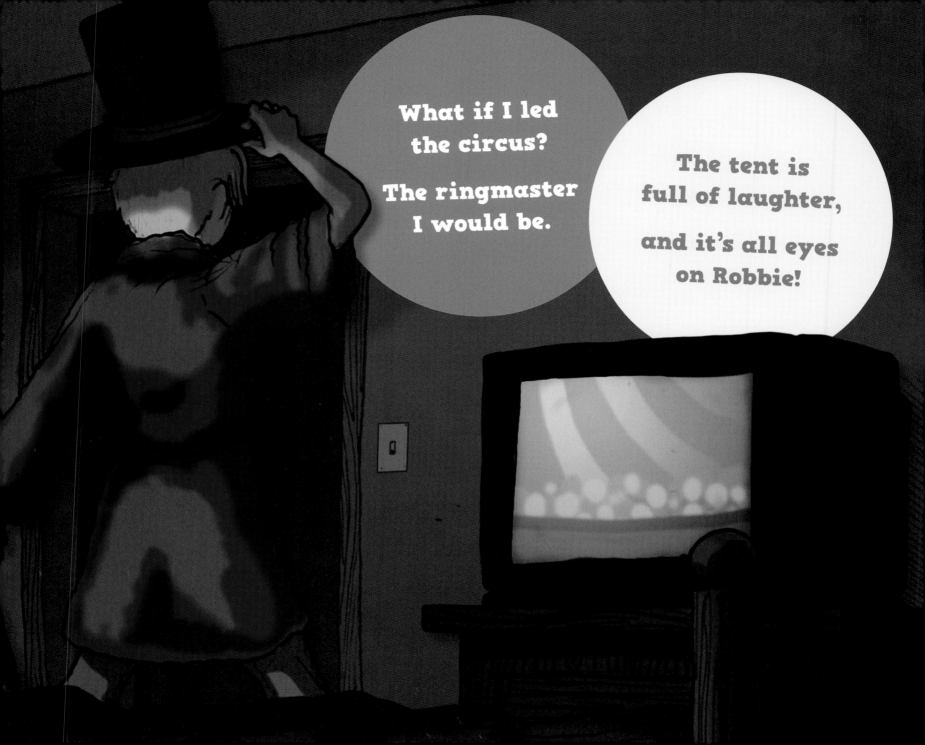

The spotlight hits the center ring
and the crowd begins to cheer.

In come the fearsome lions,
they snarl and they sneer.

Gary Cook's first published children's book, *The Best Saturday Ever*, was inspired by a painting that was purchased at an art fair and is now hanging on the wall over his desk. He is a self-employed commercial photographer doing advertising and editorial photography. He also pursues his musical interests as a drummer performing with local bands. Gary and his partner, Amy, live in Bloomington, Minnesota, with their pets, including Sparky the dog.

Adam Sward is a Minneapolis-based illustrator and tattooist. He also does graphic design, murals, live art, and some stand-up comedy now and again. He currently lives and works in South Minneapolis, Minnesota, with his dog and an almost alarmingly large collection of misinformation.